A Mighty Elephant
In The Land Of Kachoo

Written by Tina Scotford
Illustrated by Frans Groenewald

JACANA

A mighty big elephant in the land of Kachoo
Toppled then trampled the trees in his view
With his very long trunk and his ivory tusks
He pushed the trees down from dawn until dusk

The rock dassies, monkeys and banana bats, too
Went crazy with worry about what they should do
"You've broken the marula with the seeds we like best
Get out of our forest! Stop making this mess!"

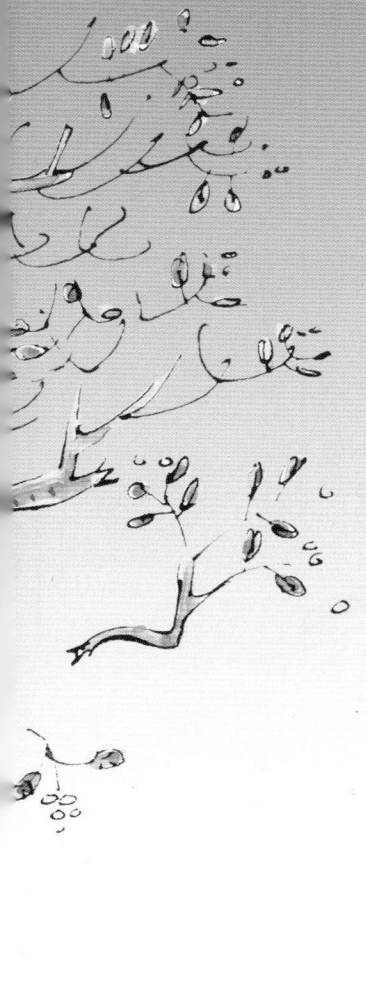

I'm saddened to hear what the bats said today
The marula I broke was just in my way
I try really hard to dodge every tree
That blocks the path in front of me

The elephant trudged on
into the wood
Squashing and squeezing
as small as he could
But as he was tall and
not very slim
Trees still fell down
because of him

The kites and the owls and the marabou storks
The raptors and eagles and black sparrow hawks
Tooted and hooted then squabbled and squawked:

"The trees that you've toppled hold up our nests!
Get out of our forest! You're making a mess!"

I'm saddened to hear what the birds said today
The knob thorn I pushed was just in my way
I try really hard with all of my might
To sidestep the trees that I see in my sight

Elephant walked towards the watering hole
While baboons steered him and stood patrol
But with a body weighing a ton plus three
He couldn't help but topple a tree

The tree fell across the watering hole
That animals used to bathe in as well
The hole was now muddy and nearly bone dry
As no rain had fallen from the African sky

The boomslang, the lizard
and the Nile crocodiles
Studied the elephant
with their thin-lipped smiles
He'd toppled the tree
that snake used as his house
Where he waited in silence to
poach a tree mouse

Sssss...

"You've broken the acacia
that I sssleep in to ressst
Elephantsss are dessstructive,
you're sssuch a pessst!
Ssseee what you've done
to my tree housse
Now where ssshall I hide
in wait for a moussse?"

Suddenly the sky crackled and rumbled
Then droplets of rain from the clouds quickly tumbled
And the tree that had fallen and lodged in the ground
Now helped to dam where the water was found

The snake, the lizard and the Nile crocodiles
Looked at elephant with wide toothy smiles
The muddy dry hole now sparkled and gleamed
With flowing blue water that freely streamed

Into the woodlands the elephant now went
Where with his long nose he picked up a scent
It smelt like the bush was burning on fire
The flames that he spotted soared even higher!

Back at the hole his nose went

DUNK!

He gathered up water
In his very long trunk

Off he sped to the firey spot
Where animals fled
from flames that were hot
The elephant trampled
the bush and the trees
So animals could flee with far greater ease

The elephant sprayed and stamped on the fire
But still the flames flicked up higher and higher

So quickly the elephant
grabbed from the trees
All the young chicks
that he could see

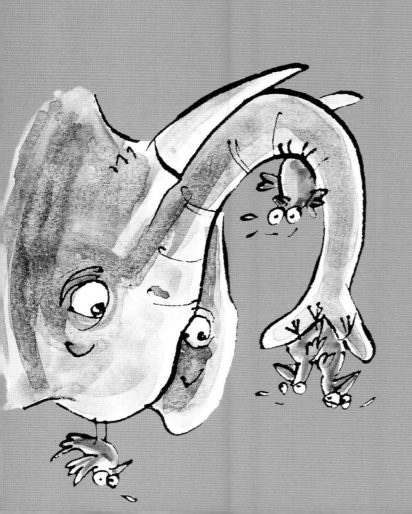

Back to the hole
the elephant raced
To gather more water
at a frantic pace

But the elephant's legs were beginning to tire
From his efforts to save Kachoo from the fire
He felt quite drained, his energy sapped
But lifted his great ears when he heard:

the DASSIES are trapped!

They're stuck in a cave
now blocked by a rock
The monkeys and bats
were frantic with shock

"Who can help unblock the cave?
We need someone strong
and really brave!"

The elephant thumped forward so mighty and brave
And ran to the entrance of the rock-blocked cave
Then using his tusks with all of his might
He rolled the big rock far out of sight

The dassies were free, they hastily fled
And back to the flames the elephant sped
Then using his flexible nose as a spout
He sprayed the hot fire and squished it all out

The kites and the owls and the marabou storks
The raptors and eagles and black sparrow hawks
Tooted and hooted and shouted:

"Thank you elephant for saving Kachoo